THE FOX MAIDEN

by Elsa Marston   illustrated by Tatsuro Kiuchi

SIMON & SCHUSTER BOOKS FOR YOUNG READERS

SIMON & SCHUSTER BOOKS FOR YOUNG READERS
An imprint of Simon & Schuster Children's Publishing Division
1230 Avenue of the Americas
New York, New York 10020
Text copyright © 1996 by Elsa Marston
Illustrations copyright © 1996 by Tatsuro Kiuchi
SIMON & SCHUSTER BOOKS FOR YOUNG READERS is a trademark of Simon & Schuster.
Book design by Lucille Chomowicz
The text of this book is set in Hiroshige Book
The illustrations are rendered in acrylics
Manufactured in the United States of America
First Edition
10 9 8 7 6 5 4 3 2 1

Library of Congress Cataloging-in-Publication Data
Marston, Elsa.
        The Fox Maiden / by Elsa Marston ; illustrated by Tatsuro Kiuchi.
                    p.   cm.
        Summary: A young fox who uses magic to change herself into human form
learns that being true to herself is the best way to live.
[1. Foxes—Fiction.   2. Magic—Fiction.   3. Self-acceptance—Fiction.]   I. Kiuchi, Tatsuro, ill.
II. Title.
PZ7.M356755Fo   1996   [E]—dc20 95-1190 CIP   AC
ISBN: 0-689-80107-6

For my friend Haruo Washi —E. M.

To my grandparents —T. K.

One spring morning long ago in Japan, a young fox went padding silently through the mountain forest. From the edge of the woods she could see a prosperous village across the valley.

She had watched the village for many days, wondering about the world of humans. Would it not be better than the simple life of the forest? There was bound to be more food, at least, for she could hear the cocks crow and the chickens cackle.

"Be careful," the older foxes had warned her. "That world is full of danger. Life in the forest may be hard and food scarce, but here you are safe."

Nevertheless, the young fox wished to learn for herself.

She did not, however, intend to prowl around the village and risk being caught by the dogs. No, she knew a better way. The foxes of the mountain possessed a remarkable secret . . . they could change themselves into human form.

Again the older foxes had cautioned her, saying the magic could not always be trusted and might have results that a fox could not foresee. But the young fox was eager to try. At the forest's edge she put aside her fox form and pulled on the ragged garments that she had found in a woodcutter's hut. Now a beautiful young woman, she walked erect the rest of the way.

As she entered the village, the dogs caught the fox maiden's scent. Though confused, they followed her, barking and snapping at her bare heels. Before long, the fox maiden became too frightened to go any farther. Would she have to return to her own world after all?

Then a strong voice rose above the snarling of the dogs. The fox maiden turned and saw a young man. With a few well-aimed stones he drove the dogs away.

"I thank you for your kindness," she said, finding speech to match her human form. "I am a stranger and seek work to help my poor family in the forest."

"Then come with me," the young man said. "My name is Haruo and I am the manservant to Agawa, the richest man in the village. Perhaps there will be work for you in his large house."

Old Agawa smiled when he saw the beautiful fox maiden, who now called herself Yuri. "Truly you are like the lily for which you are named," he said. "Yes, you may stay here." Her magic, thought Yuri, was working very well indeed!

Not everything, though, went easily. The cook ordered Yuri here and there, and as she hurried, she longed for her four swift feet. At night the thin quilt never kept her as warm as her thick fur had, in the cozy den with her brothers and sisters. And whenever a plump chicken was killed for the master's dinner, the smell nearly drove Yuri wild.

She soon discovered, however, that her small white fingers could move with a nimbleness that none of the other servants could match. She learned how to arrange flowers, take fine stitches, and prepare the most delicate foods.

When the master called on Yuri to serve him tea, she moved gracefully, silent as a shadow. Pleased, Agawa asked her to attend him and his friends in the evening. In her high, sweet voice she sang haunting songs such as no one had ever heard before, like the breeze through tall pines and the murmur of forest streams.

Sometimes Yuri caught a glimpse of Haruo listening as she sang, and his eyes held a look that she did not understand. One day he said to her, "Beauty and happiness have come to this house with you. I hope you will stay, Yuri." After that, her heart quickened when he spoke to her, and she often paused in her work to admire his skill and strength.

For a while, Yuri was content in her new life, with plenty to eat and soft fabrics to wear. But as the days went on, she began to tire of her work. Why not let people find and eat their own food, as *her* family did? And what a struggle it was to tame her long, thick hair! As for mincing about in kimono and tight slippers—why, she hadn't had a good run in ages!

More and more, Yuri's thoughts returned to her forest home. On the mountainside she would be free to do just as she pleased. Yes, she decided, she would go back to the forest for a while—and take a fat chicken for her family.

That night Yuri slipped out to the henhouse and deftly seized a chicken before it could even squawk. She hurried unseen through the empty streets and along the road to the forest. There she changed back to her own form, leaving her kimono neatly by a rock.

Reaching her home, the young fox found a joyful welcome. She raced freely among the trees, frolicking with her brothers and sisters.

Yet the fox could not forget her life among people. Before long she found herself wondering, *Does anyone ever think of me at Agawa's house? What is Haruo doing?* Finally she decided to go back, and again her family could not stop her.

As she neared the edge of the woods, however, the young fox was spotted by a hunter. She managed to conceal herself in thick underbrush until he had gone. Then, still trembling, she found the clothes she had hidden. Again the magic spell transformed her into a woman, and she made the rest of her way to the village without trouble.

When she reached Agawa's house, she found it in an uproar. "My little Yuri!" the old man cried. "Where have you been? Everything is at odds here without you."

Yuri told him that her family had needed her, but Agawa still fretted. "No, I cannot let you go away. When your family needs help, I shall send something. But you must stay here."

In the servants' quarters, Haruo spoke to her. "If you go to the forest again, Yuri, let me accompany you to keep you safe."

Yuri thanked him and busied herself with her work. Still, she could not forget the sting of Agawa's orders. And now her sharp ears began to pick up grumbling among the servants.

"A poor girl from nowhere," muttered the cook, "yet she will have nothing to do with us. She must have a secret."

"She is beautiful," sighed the stable man. "But I think she has bewitched our old master."

"She has such quick fingers—like a thief's!" whispered another maidservant. "Maybe *she* took the missing hen."

At that, Haruo said, "Enough gossip! You are envious, that's all."

At night, while the others slept, Yuri paced restlessly. The fine house now felt like a trap to her. Yet it seemed that something besides walls and Agawa's wishes held her, something she could not quite comprehend.

The next morning she heard the servants say that a fox had been glimpsed near the fields. The village men were going to take their dogs to the woods to kill all the foxes they could find. Yuri shivered. She must warn her family. Yes, it was time to leave this world, where the comfortable life hid such cruel danger.

That night, as Yuri was about to slip out of the house, she noticed Haruo asleep near the door of Agawa's room. She paused to gaze at him. Sadness filled her, for he had been kind to her, and she would never see him again. Then she left Agawa's house and hurried back to the forest, leaving her kimono by the rock as she had the first time.

Once more in her woodland home, the young fox warned the others about the hunters. They moved deeper into the forest, and soon the young fox was again romping freely with her family.

Just as before, however, she found that she could not enjoy her freedom for long. She seemed to hear Haruo's voice and see his eyes gazing intently at her. As she paced back and forth, she wondered, *Why does my heart feel such yearning? I must live in the forest and forget the foolish world of people, yet I cannot! Have I become too much a woman?*

Her family warned, "Twice you were lucky. But if you go a third time, you may never come back to us."

The young fox knew they were right, and she feared Agawa's displeasure. Finally, though, she could no longer resist her desire to return to the village. At night she set off through the forest. The sun was just rising by the time the young fox reached the rock where she had left her clothes. Once again she took the shape of a woman, dressed, and hurried among the fields to the village.

To her surprise, a dog confronted her, baring its teeth. Then others approached, until a whole pack of growling curs had gathered. People, too, stopped to stare. Some looked alarmed, others angry. As the fox maiden hastened toward the house of Agawa, a crowd followed.

She was now beside herself with fear. What could possibly be the trouble?

At Agawa's house, the servants barred her way. She begged them to call Agawa, but when the old man appeared and saw her, his face grew dark.

"Get out, get out!" he shouted. "Evil creature of the forest, you tricked me by magic! Be off with you!"

As she turned away in despair, the fox maiden looked down—and at last she saw what had happened. This time the magic had betrayed her. From beneath her fine kimono there still dragged the bushy tail of a mountain fox.

She started to run back through the village, the crowd at her heels. Dogs rushed after her, snarling and snapping. Hampered by her garments, the fox maiden stumbled and fell, sure that this would be the end of her.

Just then, she heard a familiar voice. Haruo's strong hand pulled the fox maiden to her feet. With the crowd shouting curses at them both, they fled together through the village. At last they escaped and ran across the fields toward the forest, the angry villagers and their dogs not far behind.

Only when Haruo and the fox maiden reached a spot deep inside the woods did they dare to rest. But Haruo still held her by the hand. Desperate for the safety of her forest home, the fox maiden struggled.

"Let me go now!" she begged. "I shall never return to your treacherous world."

"You, too," he said, "have deceived!"

Startled, the fox maiden grew still for a moment. "Then why did you want to save me?" she asked.

Haruo gazed at her, then spoke simply. "Because I loved you. No matter what you may be, no matter what might happen to me, I could not let you be hurt."

As the fox maiden looked up into Haruo's eyes, her wild heart understood at last what she had always seen there—and why she had had to return to his world.

Just at that moment, the sound of barking dogs again reached them. Haruo glanced in fear behind him and around at the forbidding wilderness. Then, with a sigh he released the fox maiden, saying, "Go now, and you will be safe. Hurry!"

The forest beckoned to her on every side. In the blink of an eye she could slip among the trees, vanish into the shadows, and be gone forever from the world of humans. Yet though the barking grew closer, the fox maiden did not run. The words from Haruo's heart had worked their magic, and she could never again be the simple creature she once had been.

"No," she said, "I'll not leave you now, for you can neither stay here nor return to your village. If you will follow, I shall help you find another home."

She let the tattered silk kimono drop to the ground and took her true form. Along secret paths, the young fox led Haruo through the dense forest. Across the mountain they traveled until, at day's end, they reached a distant valley where the roofs of a village could be seen in the evening mist.

At the forest's edge, the young fox gazed at Haruo for the last time, her heart filled with longing. Then she turned and fled back into the darkness.